Usborne English Readers

Level 1

Rapunzel

Retold by Laura Cowan

Illustrated by Sara Gianassi

English language consultant: Peter Viney

Contents

You can listen to the story online here:
www.usborneenglishreaders.com/
rapunzel

A beautiful woman was sitting in her kitchen. She was going to have a baby. She wanted to eat all kinds of strange things. She ate cheese with cake, and meat with apples, but she was still hungry.

One day, she said "I need to eat salad leaves. I'd really like some rapunzel."

"I'm sorry, but we don't have any rapunzel in our garden," said her husband.

"There's some in Madam Gothel's garden," said the woman, "Bring me some, please! I don't feel well," she complained.

"But Madam Gothel is a witch!" said her husband. "We can't take her rapunzel."

That night, he climbed over the garden
wall anyway and looked around. Madam
Gothel wasn't at home. He took a few
rapunzel leaves and ran back to his wife.

"Oh, thank you!" she said. She ate the
leaves and felt much better.

Every day, the man climbed over the wall and took some more leaves. A week later, he heard a voice. "So you're stealing my rapunzel! How can I punish you?"

It was Madam Gothel, and she was angry. "Please, my wife isn't well. I took it for her. She's going to have a baby. She needs it," said the man.

"Well, then," said the witch, "you must pay me for it. You must give me your baby."

The man fell on his knees. "No, don't take our child," he whispered.

His wife cried and cried, but she and her husband were frightened of Madam Gothel. A few months later, the witch came and took the baby. "I'm going to call her Rapunzel, like the leaves!" she said, and she laughed.

In a few years, the baby was a beautiful little girl with golden-brown hair, just like her mother. In a few years more, Madam Gothel started to worry. "Stay inside the house," she said. "You're safe here with me. Nobody can take you away."

Then, when Rapunzel was twelve years old, the witch put her in a tall tower in the middle of the forest. There were no doors or stairs, just one window at the top.

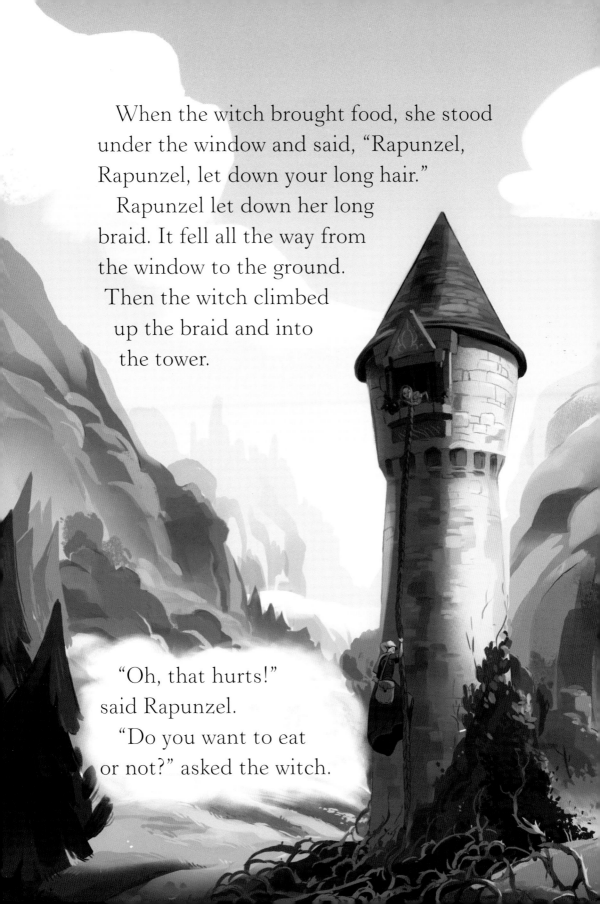

When the witch brought food, she stood
under the window and said, "Rapunzel,
Rapunzel, let down your long hair."
Rapunzel let down her long
braid. It fell all the way from
the window to the ground.
Then the witch climbed
up the braid and into
the tower.

"Oh, that hurts!"
said Rapunzel.
"Do you want to eat
or not?" asked the witch.

For many years, Rapunzel was alone all day. She had no friends, and she never left the tower, so she was often bored. She liked singing and she had a beautiful voice.

One day, a prince was riding through the forest. When he heard Rapunzel's voice, he stopped his horse. "Who is that?" he asked.

The prince rode closer until he found the tower. He couldn't see a door or stairs, or any other way in. He rode sadly home.

He went back and listened to the singing every day. One afternoon, he saw Madam Gothel near the tower. He stood behind a tree and watched her. The witch looked up to the window above and said, "Rapunzel, Rapunzel, let down your long hair."

A long braid fell to the ground and the witch climbed up it. "Aha!" thought the prince. "I can try that tomorrow."

The next afternoon, the prince rode back to the tower. "Rapunzel, Rapunzel, let down your long hair," he said. Again the long braid fell from the window, and the prince climbed up.

When she saw him, Rapunzel was very surprised. "You're not Madam Gothel!"

"No, I'm not. I listen to your beautiful singing every day. I just wanted to meet you."

Rapunzel smiled. "You're very kind," she said. And handsome, she thought.

"I would like to see you again," said the prince. "Can I come back tomorrow?"

Rapunzel smiled some more. "Oh yes, I'd like that," she said. After that, the prince came to the tower every afternoon, and Rapunzel was never bored.

One day, Madam Gothel was climbing up Rapunzel's hair and she pulled it too hard. "Ow, my head!" Rapunzel complained. "Why can't you be more careful, like the prince? He never hurts me."

When Madam Gothel climbed through
the window, she was very angry. "Who is
this prince?" she shouted.

"He's my only friend, Madam Gothel,"
whispered Rapunzel, "He comes here
every day and we talk."

"You wicked girl!" shouted the witch.
"I'm going to punish you both!"

She pulled Rapunzel's braid and cut it
off. She used a strong magic spell and sent
Rapunzel far away. Then she waited.

When the prince came back that afternoon, Madam Gothel was still in the tower. "Rapunzel, Rapunzel, let down your long hair," he called.

Madam Gothel let down Rapunzel's braid, and the prince started to climb. When he saw the witch at the window, he said "You're not my Rapunzel!"

"No, I'm not – and you're never going to see her again!" the witch laughed. She pushed the prince, and he fell all the way down into some thorns under the tower. The thorns cut his eyes, and he was blind.

"I am going to look for Rapunzel, and you can't stop me. I love her more than anything," he cried.

"You can never find her now!" shouted Madam Gothel.

The prince started walking. In every
town and in every village, he asked people
about Rapunzel. Nobody could tell him
anything about her, but he didn't stop
looking. He walked for months, until he
was far away from the forest.

One morning he heard some beautiful
singing. He knew that voice well.

"Rapunzel, is that you?" he called.

The singing stopped. "My prince!
Can it be?"

"Yes, it's me, Rapunzel. I am blind, but
I found you. After all this time, I found
you." He fell on his knees.

Rapunzel started to cry, and
her tears fell into his eyes.

"I can see! I'm not blind anymore. I can see my beautiful Rapunzel again," the prince said. He stood up and put his arms around her. Now he was crying too.

Together they walked back to the prince's home. Everyone was excited when they saw their lost prince with the lovely Rapunzel. Soon Rapunzel and the prince were married.

Rapunzel never
wanted long hair again.
She had short hair and
she was very happy.

What happened to the
witch? Nobody knows. Maybe
she is still in the tower with
Rapunzel's long braid.

About the story

Jacob and Wilhelm Grimm were brothers. They lived in Germany two hundred years ago. Together they collected and told lots of stories, like *Hansel and Gretel, Snow White* and *Rapunzel.*

Rapunzel is a fairy tale – a story about magic. Fairy tales don't always have fairies in them, but they often have princes and princesses. Before *Rapunzel,* there were a few other fairy tales about a girl in a tower. They came from France, Italy and Persia (modern-day Iran).

When the Brothers Grimm wrote their story, rapunzel was a popular vegetable in Europe. People ate the leaves and the roots, the part under the ground. Today, most people only know rapunzel because of the story.

Activities

The answers are on page 32.

Talk about people in the story

Choose the right word for each person.

1. Rapunzel's
mother is...

tired

hungry

2. Rapunzel
is...

beautiful

excited

3. The prince
is...

quiet

kind

4. Madam
Gothel is...

busy

angry

What happened when?

Can you put the pictures and sentences in order?

A.

The prince came to the tower every afternoon.

B.

"I am going to look for Rapunzel."

C.

"You must give me your baby," said the witch.

D.

"I can see my beautiful Rapunzel again."

E.

When Rapunzel was twelve years old, the witch put her in a tall tower.

F.

Madam Gothel pulled Rapunzel's braid and cut it off.

What happens next?

Choose the correct sentence.

1. A man steals rapunzel leaves from Madam Gothel.

A. Madam Gothel asks to meet his wife.

B. Madam Gothel finds him and is angry.

2. The prince sees Madam Gothel at the tower.

A. The prince climbs up Rapunzel's hair.

B. Madam Gothel shouts at him.

3. Madam Gothel waits for the prince.

A. She gives him Rapunzel's braid.

B. She pushes him out of the window.

What do they want?

Choose one thing for each person.

A.
I want to find Rapunzel.

B.
I want to eat salad leaves.

C.
I want to punish Rapunzel and the prince.

D.
I want to see the prince again.

1. Rapunzel's mother

2. Madam Gothel

3. The prince

4. Rapunzel

Rapunzel, Rapunzel

One word in each sentence is wrong.
Can you choose the right word instead?

1.

Rapunzel never left the village
so she was often bored.

dogs garden tower

2.

"He's my only teacher, Madam
Gothel," whispered Rapunzel.

father friend horse

3.

"Ow, my breakfast,"
complained Rapunzel.

feet hair head

4.

She had short skirts and she
was very happy.

books children hair

Word list

alone (adj) without other people.

blind (adj) if you are blind, you can't see anything.

bored (adj) when you don't have anything interesting to do, you are bored.

braid (n) a way of wearing long hair so that it is twisted together like a rope.

complain (v) when you are not happy about something and you say so, you complain.

handsome (adj) (*about a man*) good-looking.

kind (adj) good and nice to other people.

knee (n) the part that bends in the middle of your leg.

leaf, leaves (n) trees and plants have leaves. Most leaves are green. Some leaves turn yellow, red and brown in the autumn.

let down (v) to make something fall down, usually when you are still holding a part of it.

punish (v) you might punish someone for doing something bad, usually by taking away something nice or something that they want.